Guy Parker-Rees

DYLAN
THE BAKER

Hello, I'm Dotty Bug. Let's join in with the story!

ALISON GREEN BOOKS

When it's a sunny day,
Dylan's ready to play.

But what kind of day was
it today? A lolling about,
not-doing-very-much
kind of day?

No way!

"Today," said Dylan, "is a day for being a baker. It's Jolly Otter's birthday, and *I* have promised to bake him a cake!"

Dylan dived under his bed,
rummaged around, and found . . .

Have YOU ever baked a cake?

... his chef's hat and apron, and a big, shiny baking tin.

He opened his kitchen cupboard and found:

"Hooray!" said Dylan. "I can make my favourite Choccy-Banana cake."

While Dylan baked, he sang his Cakey-Bakey song:

"I'm going to bake a cake,
A cake is what I'll bake,

I'll whisk it
and crack it,

I'll sift it and bash it,

I'm going to bake a cake."

What's YOUR
favourite cake?

He mixed everything together, dolloped it into
the tin, and carefully put it in the hot oven.

It took ages to cook.

And it smelled so delicious that

Dylan's tummy started to rumble.

Rumble-grumble!

Does YOUR tummy rumble when you're hungry?

But at last the oven went, "Ping!"
and the cake was ready!

I want
a nibble!

It smelled absolutely scrumptious.

Dylan was just about to eat
some, when he remembered:

"Oh, no!

It's Jolly Otter's birthday cake!
I'm not allowed."

But it was too hard, looking
at the cake and not eating it.
So he ran outside to do
something else instead.

Dylan was busy doing headstands
when Purple Puss and Titchy Chick passed by.
"What are you doing, Dylan?" asked Purple Puss.
"I'm trying not to eat cake," said Dylan.

"I'll help," said Purple Puss.
"Cheep," said Titchy Chick, which meant she wanted to help, too.

Can YOU do a headstand?

So they all tried not to eat cake together.
But the smell of the cake kept wafting
round their noses, and their tummies
started to rumble:

Rumble-grumble
RUMBLE!

"It smells so nice!" said Purple Puss.
"Can't we just have a little slice?"

What's YOUR favourite smell?

"No!" said Dylan. "We're not allowed.
It's Jolly Otter's birthday cake."
"Then we have to go much further away,"
said Purple Puss, "and do something else instead."

So they ran to the woods
and started spinning round in circles.
But the smell of the cake wafted all the way
to the woods, and their tummies rumbled
even louder:

Rumbly-tumbly-grumbly-GRUM!

Can YOU spin round in circles?

Titchy Chick couldn't wait any longer.
"Cheep!" she whimpered, which meant,
"Can we eat the cake NOW?"

"**No!**" cried Dylan. "We're not allowed!
It's Jolly Otter's birthday cake."
"Then we have to go **really** far away,"
said Purple Puss, "and do something else instead."

So they splashed
through the stream.

They swung on
the big swing.

Have YOU swung on
a swing today?

They balanced
on the wobbly log.

They puffed to the top of the hill.
But now they were even hungrier,
and their tummies were rumbling
even more loudly:

Rumbly-tumbly-grumbly-
GRUM!

"What shall we
do now?" said Dylan.

Do YOU like racing?

"I know!" said Purple Puss.
"Race you back to Dylan's house!"

And, before they knew it, they'd
raced all the way home . . .

... and eaten up

all the cake!

It tasted really good.

But then Dylan remembered: "Oh, no!
It's time for Jolly Otter's party,
and we've eaten all of
his cake!"

"You'll just have to give him the empty tin instead," said Purple Puss.

They all trudged sadly off to Jolly Otter's boat.

Uh-oh! What will Jolly Otter say?

Jolly Otter was very excited about his party.
"Is that my cake?" he said.

Do YOU think
Jolly Otter will
like his present?

"It WAS your cake," said Dylan. "But we ate it by mistake."
He gave Jolly Otter the cake tin.

Jolly Otter looked at the empty tin.

Then he said . . .

"I love it! Now we can have a cake-baking party!"
"Hooray!" said Dylan. "I'll teach you my Cakey-Bakey song!"

Can YOU
sing along, too?

And they all sang:

"Let's all bake a cake,
A cake is what we'll bake,
We'll whisk it and crack it,
We'll sift it and bash it,
We'll wait for it to bake . . .

"And then we'll eat the cake!
Yum, yum, yum!

Happy birthday, Jolly Otter!"

Dylan's **Best Ever** Choccy-Banana Cake

1. Ask a grown-up to set the oven to 170C/325F/Gas 3.
2. Use baking parchment to line the base and sides of a deep, round, loose-bottomed 20 cm cake tin.
3. Microwave the butter for a few seconds, till it's very soft.
4. Beat the butter and sugar together in a food mixer until they're light and creamy.
5. Mix in the beaten eggs, a little bit at a time.
6. Sift in the flour, then add the vanilla extract, bananas and chocolate chips. Fold together gently with a big spoon. Try to keep lots of air in the mixture, and don't over-mix.
7. Dollop the mixture into your cake tin. Sprinkle the top with demerara sugar, and bake in the pre-heated oven for about an hour. Cover the top with foil if it browns too quickly.
8. The cake is cooked when it's nice and brown, and feels a bit springy in the middle.
9. Cool the cake on a rack. Decorate it with icing and sweets – or eat it just as it is!

Here's what you'll need:

* 175g/6oz butter
* 175g/6oz golden caster sugar
* 2 free-range eggs, lightly beaten
* 175g/6oz self-raising flour
* 2 very ripe bananas, peeled and chopped
* a drop of vanilla extract
* 175g/6oz dark or milk chocolate, bashed into little bits
* a sprinkle of demerara sugar

First published in the UK in 2018
by Alison Green Books
An imprint of Scholastic Children's Books,
Euston House, 24 Eversholt Street, London NW1 1DB
A division of Scholastic Ltd • www.scholastic.co.uk
London – New York – Toronto – Sydney – Auckland
Mexico City – New Delhi – Hong Kong
Copyright © 2018 Guy Parker-Rees
HB ISBN: 978 1 407171 75 3 • PB ISBN: 978 1 407171 76 0

For James, who likes cake,
love from Dad x